The Berenstain Bears
Save Christmas

The Berenstain Bears Save Christmas

Stan & Jan Berenstain
with Mike Berenstain

■ HARPERCOLLINS*PUBLISHERS*

The Berenstain Bears Save Christmas Copyright © 2003 by Berenstain Enterprises Printed in the U.S.A. All rights reserved. www.harperchildrens.com
Library of Congress Cataloging-in-Publication Data Berenstain, Stan, 1923– The Berenstain bears save Christmas / Stan & Jan Berenstain ; with Mike Berenstain.
p.   cm.   Summary: Thinking that the spirit of Christmas has been lost, Santa Bear disappears, until the Berenstain Bears show him that it still exists. ISBN 0-06-052670-X
— ISBN 0-06-052671-8 (lib. bdg.) [1. Christmas—Fiction.   2. Bears—Fiction.   3. Stories in rhyme.] I. Berenstain, Jan, 1923– II. Berenstain, Michael. III. Title.
PZ8.3.B4493 Bhim 2003 [E]—dc21 2002151782   Typography by Matt Adamec 1 2 3 4 5 6 7 8 9 10 ❖ First Edition

SHOP AT GRIZZLY MALL

MERRY CHRISTMAS

'Twas the month before Christmas,
    and all round the mall
the pre-Christmas traffic
had slowed to a crawl.
The stores were a-selling,
the horns were a-blowing,
the shoppers were
busily to-ing and fro-ing.

Even the family that lived
down the sunny dirt road
(for directions just ask
any chipmunk or toad)
and were usually full of
calm Christmas cheer—
they too were going
Christmas-crazy this year!

Mama Bear missed how it all used to be, when all Christmas needed was a small Christmas tree. Christmastime once was a time just for caring, a time for all families to be giving and sharing.

But now it seemed Christmas
no longer meant love.
Now it seemed Christmas
meant let's push and shove!
Let's fight for that
very last toy on the shelf!
Let's look out for that
fellow known as yourself!

But a watcher was watching
that Bear Country scene,
keeping close track of Christmas
on his scanner-machine.
And who was that watcher,
did I hear you ask?
Why, the person in charge
of the whole Christmas task!

It was Santa himself
who was watching this mess.
And what did he think?
You can probably guess.
What was happening to Christmas,
grown swollen and huge,
was turning old Santa
right into a *Scrooge!*

Santa, like Mama,
longed for Christmas of old,
when he flew through the night,
so bracingly cold,
in his magical sleigh
all laden with toys
for all the good
little cub girls and boys.
But now things had changed
and not for the better.
He used to enjoy
reading each little cub's letter.
Now Santa got e-mail,
which he read with alarm,
all asking for toys
fully lacking in charm.

"This cub wants a video game,
   and I hate to say it,
but this game is so complicated
it's easier not to play it!
And here is one that's even worse—
cubs simply do not need it—
a virtual pet that up and bites
if you fail to feed it.
And worst of all,
this cub wants this innovative cutie,
a miniature canine named
Little Doggie Dooty,
with an item purchased extra
that's positively super,
a high-tech battery-operated
electronic pooper-scooper."

Santa Bear was angry,
upset, and annoyed.
"If things don't change," he thundered,
"Christmas will be null and void!"
And depressed and discouraged,
he jumped into his bed,
turned out all the lights,
and pulled the covers over his head.

Meanwhile, look at what was happening
on the Bear family's street.
Christmas had become a chance
for all bears to compete!
You have never seen such gaggles
of winking blinking lights
or such a loud and rude display
of un-Christmasy sounds and sights:

Great big plastic Santas
that were roaring "Ho! Ho! Ho!,"
a whole entire house
that was wrapped with a bow,
gigantic candy canes
reaching for the sky,
speakers blaring Christmas hits
at neighbors passing by,

Reindeer whose red noses
would put Rudolph's nose to shame.
The bears, one and all,
had been caught up in the game.
All of them were trying
for the best Christmas display.
All of them were trying
to turn nighttime into day.

MY LIST~
SISTER
1. Bearbie doll
2. 10-speed bike
3. Doll-house
4. Talking Teddy
5. Playstation
6. Giant slinky
7. Pogo-stick
8. Gumball machine
9. Portable TV
10. Tape deck
11. Makeup Kit
12. Tennis racquet
13. Hockey stick
14. Mr. Potato head
15. Bead set
16. Art supplies
17. Walkie-talkie
18. Zoo set
19. Play
20.

MY LIST~
BROTHER
1. Videocam
2. Guitar
3. Electric train
4. Tether plane
5. Action figures
6. CD player
7. Football helmet
8. Roller blades
9. Baseball glove
10. Basket-ball
11. Skate-board
12. Monopoly game
13. Magic kit
14. Remote-control car
15. Dinosaur set
16. Computer
17. C.D. Burner
Rates ons

The cubs were also caught up
in this nasty Christmas rage.
Their Christmas wish list
grew to cover page after page.
Mama Bear tried her best
to pull Pa from the brink.
She begged him, please,
to take a moment just to stop and think.
But Papa, like the cubs,
was still carried quite away.
There was no doubt the greedies
would spoil Christmas Day!

Now Mrs. Santa loved Christmas
just as much as her mate.
She especially liked the catalog
that came from Bearal and Crate.
But she too thought that Christmas
had gotten out of hand
and that the Christmas greedies
were spreading through the land.

She was worried about Christmas,
but worried more about her mate.
Hot tea usually cheered him up,
with fresh-baked cookies on a plate.
But Santa Bear was gone!
There was just a note on the bed.
It was pinned to Santa's pillow,
and this is what it said:

Subject: Christmas is Canceled!
To my dear and loving wife,
Christmas is my life,
and what I have to say
is that the true spirit of Christmas
has somehow lost its way.
I have gone to find it.
I will search until I do.
But better that there's none at all
than what it's turned into.

Your loving husband

Of course Santa's disappearance
made the network news.
Folks gathered round their TV screens
in fours and threes and twos.
They called up all the talk shows
and all said, "What a shame!"
But not a single bear thought
the bears were to blame.

Mama Bear knew better.
"Of course Santa Bear has quit!
And with all that's happened,
you can't blame him a bit!
We've blotted out the stars
with a million watts of light.
We have lost the Christmas spirit
and forgotten all that's right."

The bears knew in their heart of hearts
that Mama Bear was right,
and that they had all contributed
to Christmas's sad plight.
The bear cubs got the message,
and Papa Bear did, too.
But what was done was done, they thought,
and what were they to do?

"Well," said Mama Bear,
        "we could set a good example.
I think a few lights around the door
will be more than ample."
So Papa and the cubs saw
the error of their ways
and, working very quickly,
they took down the huge displays.
But Santa was still missing,
when all was said and done,
and the chance of saving Christmas
seemed clearly slim to none.

But Santa had a plan,
and he was really still about.
And with the fate of Christmas
still very much in doubt,
he went among the bears
very carefully disguised,
and traveling without his sleigh
he went unrecognized.

So in his tweedy cap and suit,
he traveled far and wide,
and looking for the Christmas spirit,
he searched the countryside.
He had to keep on searching;
he could not give up hope.
Hmm, this place looked familiar.
He had seen it on his scope!
Santa looked up at the stars
sparkling in the sky.
No longer did the lights below
outshine the lights on high.
Well, that's a start, thought Santa,
with a hopeful smile.
Maybe my long, lonely search
will finally prove worthwhile.

But Santa needed more than
just soft lights around the door.
He needed the true spirit of Christmas
back in place once more.
Santa still worried
about Christmas and its fate.
And then he checked his watch,
which showed the time, the day, the date.
And with alarm he cried out loud,
"Good grief! It's Christmas Eve!"
Was there still time enough
for Christmas's reprieve?

Santa knew full well
that it was about to snow.
He could always feel it coming
in his left big toe.
But suddenly it was snowing
with all of nature's might.
It whipped and whirled and swirled.
It whited out the night.
It crystallized the air.
It filled the very skies!
It was as if the air
were filled with icy fireflies.

Then at that very moment,
through the whirling, swirling snow,
far off in the distance,
he saw a gentle glow.
Despite the cold and blowing snow,
he could clearly see
that the light he saw before him
came from the Bears' big tree.
The very same Bear family
he had seen upon his scope.
The very same Bear family
who had made him give up hope.

Just then the door opened,
and there was Papa Bear
coming out into the cold
from his warm and cozy lair.
Out he came so bravely
through the deep and drifting snow,
even though the windchill
was eighty-six below.

P apa had a cup of birdseed
and a tiny holly wreath.
And he pressed forward further
into the blizzard's icy teeth.
Papa had come out to feed a tiny bird
no bigger than a mouse,
a tiny hungry bird
in a tiny cold birdhouse.
Pa hung the wreath
and placed the cup under the eaves,
safe beneath the shelter
of snow-laden leaves.

Santa said to Papa,
"What a nice thing to do."
"Not at all," said Papa.
"Little birdies gotta eat on Christmas, too.
But if you don't mind my asking,
who the heck are you?"
"Er—Yule's the name," said Santa.
"Just a stranger passing through."
"Well, whoever you are," said Papa,
"'tain't fit out for bear or beast.
So come in and get warm.
I can't offer you a feast,
but Mama's Christmas cocoa
is the best warmer-upper.
And we would be so tickled
if you would stay for supper."

So Santa Bear and Papa Bear
came in from the cold.
And then Santa saw Christmas
as it was in days of old.
There was a fresh-cut tree,
paper stars on the windowpanes,
and all around the room
were homemade paper chains.
Santa's search had ended,
and his spirit was more than buoyed.
Santa Bear was more than pleased.
He was overjoyed!

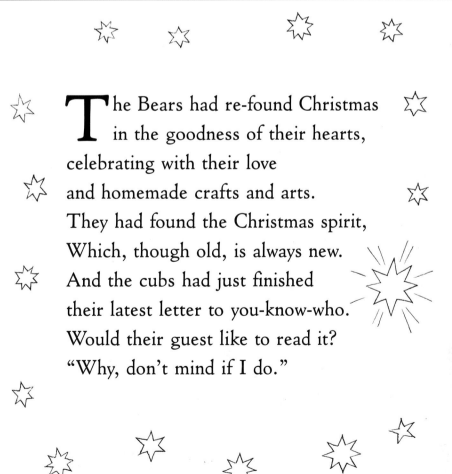

The Bears had re-found Christmas
in the goodness of their hearts,
celebrating with their love
and homemade crafts and arts.
They had found the Christmas spirit,
Which, though old, is always new.
And the cubs had just finished
their latest letter to you-know-who.
Would their guest like to read it?
"Why, don't mind if I do."

Santa quick put on his specs
and read the cubs' brief note.
As he read it, he got quite
a lump inside his throat.
The letter did not ask
for every greedy Christmas whim.
It left the matter of gifts
for them completely up to him.

It requested gifts for others:
a toy mouse for Miz McGrizz's cat,
a plant for Miz McGrizz herself,
and for Mailbear Bill, a hat,
something nice for Grizzly Gus,
who had had a fall.
As gifts for themselves—again,
that was Santa's call.
A great big smile spread slowly
across old Santa's face.
Yes, the true Christmas spirit
was alive in this warm place.

After supper Pa looked out
and said, "The snow has slowed."
So they left the Bears' house
and went down a snowy road.
It was a lovely cold night
with the snow still gently falling
as the Bear family and their guest
went a-Christmas calling.
They exchanged small gifts among themselves
and warm homemade dishes,
and happy and heartwarming
merry Christmas wishes.

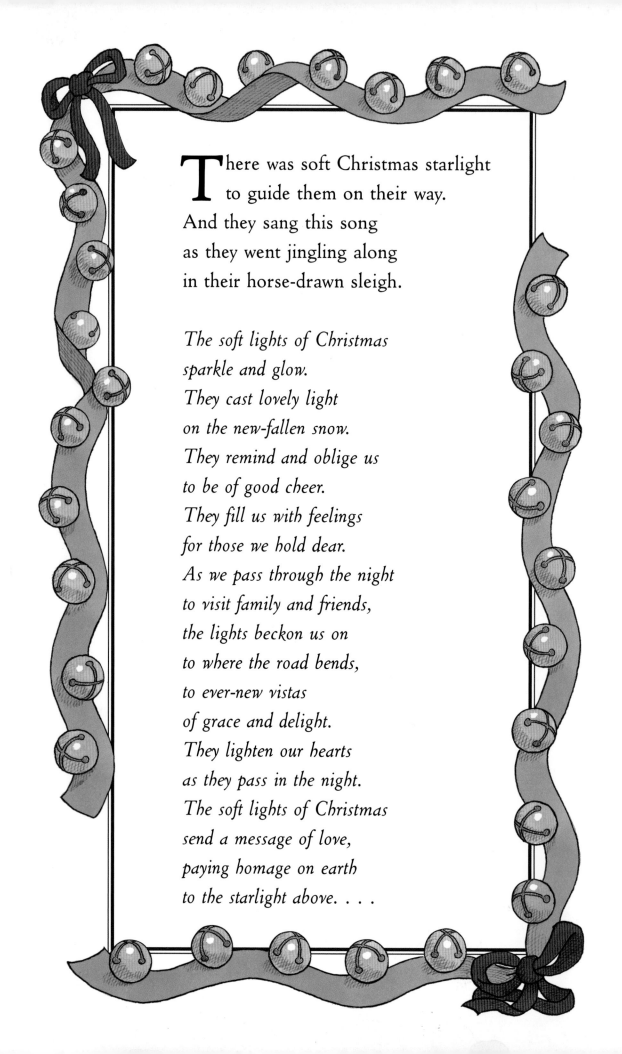

There was soft Christmas starlight
to guide them on their way.
And they sang this song
as they went jingling along
in their horse-drawn sleigh.

The soft lights of Christmas
sparkle and glow.
They cast lovely light
on the new-fallen snow.
They remind and oblige us
to be of good cheer.
They fill us with feelings
for those we hold dear.
As we pass through the night
to visit family and friends,
the lights beckon us on
to where the road bends,
to ever-new vistas
of grace and delight.
They lighten our hearts
as they pass in the night.
The soft lights of Christmas
send a message of love,
paying homage on earth
to the starlight above. . . .

Merry Christmas!

"Thanks for the lift. Now I must leave,"
    said old Santa Bear.
"Here's where you can let me off.
I'm staying over there."
And with a wink and a twinkle
he bid them all good-bye.
And then he was off like magic
through the Christmas Eve sky.
"I have searched for Christmas!" he cried.
"And found the Spirit True.
Now if you'll excuse me,
I have work to do."